For Georgia,
the girl with the dancing feet.

PEACHTREE PUBLISHERS
1700 Chattahoochee Avenue
Atlanta, Georgia 30318-2112
www.peachtree-online.com

Text and illustrations © 2013 by Alex T. Smith

First published in the United Kingdom in 2013 by Hodder Children's Books
First United States version published in 2015 by Peachtree Publishers

Artwork created digitally. Title is hand lettered;
text is typeset in Italian Garamond BT.

Printed and bound in April 2015 in China by RR Donnelley & Sons

10 9 8 7 6 5 4 3 2 1
First Edition

Library of Congress Cataloging-in-Publication Data

Smith, Alex T.
  Claude in the spotlight / Alex T. Smith.
     pages cm
  ISBN 978-1-56145-895-0
  Summary: Claude the dog and his sidekick, a sock named Sir Bobblysock, join a
dance act competing in a variety show for a delicious prize: unlimited cakes from
Mr. Lovelybuns's Bakery.
  [1. Dogs—Fiction. 2. Socks—Fiction. 3. Dance—Fiction. 4. Humorous stories.]
I. Title.
  PZ7.S6422Cm 2015
  [Fic]—dc23
                            2015006622

CLAUDE

in the Spotlight

ALEX T. SMITH

PEACHTREE
ATLANTA

Chapter 1

Behind a red front door with a big brass knocker lives a little dog named Claude. And here he is!

hello !

fancy red beret

stylish red sweater

well-polished shoes

Claude is a small dog.
Claude is a small, plump dog.
Claude is a small, plump dog
who wears a fancy red beret
and a stylish red sweater.

Claude's owners are Mr. and Mrs. Shinyshoes and his best friend is Sir Bobblysock.

Sir Bobblysock is both a sock and quite bobbly.

Every morning, Mr. and Mrs.
Shinyshoes wave good-bye to Claude
and set off for work. And that is
when the fun begins. Where will
Claude and Sir Bobblysock go today?

Chapter 2

One day, shortly after Mr. and Mrs. Shinyshoes had rushed out the door, Claude leaped out of bed with a spring in his step, dislodging Sir Bobblysock's hairnet and almost knocking over his cup of tea.

Claude should have been feeling rather sleepy because the night before he had stayed up *very* late (until about half past eight) reading a book of ghost stories.

Some of the ghosts were spooky
looking. Claude was especially worried
about how they floated around and
didn't wear any shoes.

But that was last night.
Now Claude was wide awake
with his beret on, looking for
something to do.

"I think I will go for a walk
into town," he said. And he did.

Sir Bobblysock decided to go too. Really his hair needed washing, but he felt that no good would come of him lounging around all day with his head wrapped up in a towel, so the two friends set off.

Suddenly, a group of
children walked by.

They were wearing
some funny outfits.
Very funny indeed…

Claude's nose tingled, his eyebrows wiggled, and his bottom waggled. There was *definitely* an adventure brewing here!

Quickly smoothing down his ears, Claude ran after the children with Sir Bobblysock hopping along behind.

Chapter 3

They followed the children into a big, bright room. There was a tall upright piano in one corner and an old lady sitting at it, playing a very jolly tune.

Claude was just about to ask if
he could play a little ditty when
the classroom door flew open.

Into the room leaped an extraordinary-looking woman!

"Good morning, everybody!" the lady boomed. "My name is Miss Henrietta Highkick-Spin, and I'm your teacher. Now come along, everyone, let's daaaaance!"

It all looked a bit too much for Sir Bobblysock (who had his knees to consider), so he went and lay on the top of the piano.

"First," called Miss Highkick-Spin, "we must warm up our bodies!" and she began skipping around and doing all sorts of strange stretches.

Claude found the skipping very easy indeed and he enjoyed the breeze around his ears as he galloped across the room.

The stretches, however, were a different matter.

Claude found that his tummy got in the way.

After everyone was nice and warm,
Miss Highkick-Spin taught the
class a gentle dance routine.

There was some more skipping
around, some leg wagging, and
some "waving-your-arms-above-
your-head-and-pretending-you-
are-a-daisy-in-a-windy-meadow."

Claude tried really hard to join in,
but when it came to the arm waving,
his paws got knotted in his ears.

"Don't worry," said Miss Highkick-Spin. "Ballet's not for everyone. Let's try some tap!" And she handed Claude some exciting new shoes.

Claude put them on and thought he looked lovely. When he walked, the shoes made a wonderful *TAP TAP TAP* noise on the floor. He showed them to Sir Bobblysock, who said they were great, but complained that he felt one of his headaches coming on.

Miss Highkick-Spin was just about to teach the class a noisy new dance when something happened...

A tiny fly, who had seen Claude waving his arms above his head and pretending to be a daisy in a windy meadow...

...flew up Claude's sweater!

It tickled.
Claude couldn't help himself.

He skittered and
jittered across the room.

He leaped and dived
high up into the air.

He wiggled and
jiggled all over until
he was almost a blur.

Sir Bobblysock
needed a big cup
of tea from just
looking at him.

Soon, the whole room was copying Claude's wiggly, jiggly dancing.

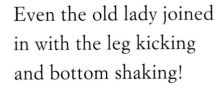

Even the old lady joined in with the leg kicking and bottom shaking!

30

Eventually the fly got bored,
escaped from Claude's sweater,
and disappeared out the window.

Claude came to a standstill.

Chapter 4

"P hew!" panted the dance teacher, pink in the face. "What a wonderful new dance! You *must* join us for the show we are performing in at the theater this afternoon! Will you?"

Claude didn't want to ask what a theater was, so he just smoothed his sweater over his tummy and nodded politely.

About an hour later, after the children had eaten their packed lunches and Claude and Sir Bobblysock had finished the emergency picnic that Claude always kept under his beret, the whole class set off for the theater.

THEATER →

This Afternoon Only!

The VARIETY SHOW

AMAZING ACTS! DARING FEATS!
WORLD FAMOUS PERFORMERS!
AND A SPECIAL
GRAND PRIZE!

33

On the way, one of the girls explained to Claude all about the show they would soon be starring in. It was going to be a variety show.

"That means lots of different people do different things on the stage," said the girl. "We will be doing your new dance! And the most exciting thing is that today, the best act wins a grand prize—all the cakes you can eat from Mr. Lovelybuns's Bakery. He's judging the competition."

Claude clapped his paws together
and Sir Bobblysock let out
a happy sigh.

Mr. Lovelybuns's Bakery was
Claude's favorite shop. Even
Sir Bobblysock, who could be
quite picky with his pastries, had
declared that Mr. Lovelybuns had
the nicest buns he'd ever seen.

Unfortunately, in the excitement, nobody saw a suspicious-looking man listening in on their conversation...

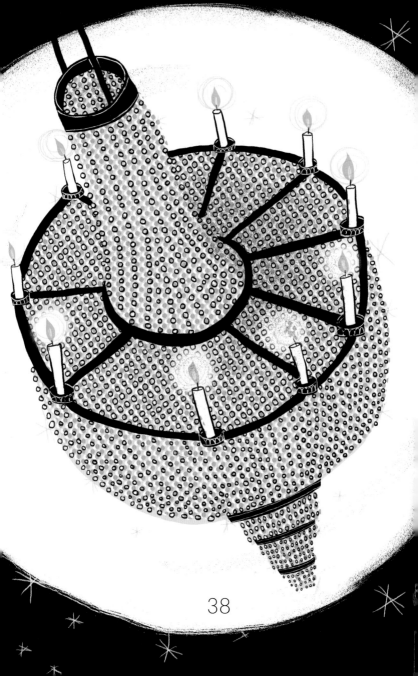

Once inside, Claude and Sir
Bobblysock liked the theater
immediately. Sir Bobblysock
liked the glitz and glamour of
the whole place.

High above the audience's
seats was a big, sparkly
chandelier. Sir Bobblysock
said that you wouldn't want
that falling on your head.
Claude nodded in agreement,
then everyone went
backstage.

Claude couldn't believe how different it was. It was dark and dusty and rather spooky.

"This is just the sort of place a ghost would live." Claude shivered, remembering his book of ghosties at home.

FRAGILE

HAS ANYONE
SEEN MY
TROUSERS?
*THE CLASSIC
TRAGEDY*
starring Sidney Thomas
* * * *

BILLY BONGO
in
Who's
Afraid of
Virginia Woof?
* * * *   * * * *

Harriet J. Harmon
in
THE SMASH HIT
Hello
SAILORS!
*****

THE INTERNATIONALLY
ACCLAIMED MUSICAL
PUSSYCATS
starring Corinne Gotch
LIMITED RUN! BOOK NOW!

1.

THE
DANC
DIVA
DAN
TROU

And he and Sir
Bobblysock quickly
hurried along to
the brightly lit
dressing rooms.

41

In the first room they found a
troupe of ladies who would be
doing a dance routine too. Sir
Bobblysock couldn't take his eyes
off their extraordinary costumes.

In the next room was The Marvellous
Marvin, a magician.

Claude and Sir Bobblysock watched
in amazement as he waved his magic
wand around and produced three tiny
rabbits from his hat.

Then Claude gave it a try…

In the final dressing room was an enormous woman dressed as a Viking.

Her special trick was singing
so high and loud that she could
shatter a teacup. Claude and
Sir Bobblysock put on the safety
goggles that Claude always kept
under his beret and watched
as the Viking demonstrated.

AAAAAAA!!!

Claude was very impressed.
Sir Bobblysock just pursed his lips.
What a way to treat a teacup!

Of course, Claude couldn't wait to give it a shot, but as hard as he tried, the glass vase wouldn't budge.

Eventually Sir Bobblysock slyly elbowed it off the table.

Claude was enjoying a pre-show
cookie when there came a shout
from down the hall...

Chapter 5

The Marvellous Marvin was standing in front of the dressing room, looking very pale.

"A g-g-g-ghost just jumped out at me and tried to snatch my magic wand," he said shakily. "It's broken, look!"

He held up the wand. It was all bent and limp like a sad sock.

"The theater ghost!" said Miss Highkick-Spin dramatically. "Every theater has a ghost, but I've never heard of one behaving so badly before."

Claude shuddered. He would have
to keep his eyes peeled for this
ghost. It was clearly trouble with a
capital *T*. Sir Bobblysock couldn't
stop his bobbles from shaking. All
this talk of ghosts had given him the
heebie-jeebies.

Before anyone could say any
more, a man with a clipboard
bustled through the crowd.

"Places please, everyone!" he said.
"The show is about to begin!"

Claude and Sir Bobblysock rushed
to the side of the stage to watch.

But first, they couldn't help
popping their heads through
the plush red curtain
to look at the audience.

Directly underneath
the big chandelier
was Mr. Lovelybuns.

He was sitting at a special judging table and looking very important. Claude waved and Mr. Lovelybuns waved back.

Suddenly, the orchestra started up and the show began.

The dancing ladies were halfway through their hot shoe shuffle when the ghost leaped out from the darkness and terrified them. One by one, they all fell over.

The last dancer tumbled into
the orchestra pit and got
her head stuck
in a tuba.

The Marvellous Marvin was no
better. His wonky wand didn't
work at all. Instead of making
a big puff of smoke come out
of his hat, he set it on fire.
Claude had to rush onto the
stage with his beret full of
water to put it out.

The audience groaned. The
show was an absolute disaster!

Soon it was Claude's turn to take to the stage. Sir Bobblysock watched from the wings.

Claude shuffled on
with the other dancers
and when the music
started, he nervously
wiggled and jiggled around.

All of a sudden, Claude
heard the stomping of
shoes behind him.

He spun around on the spot
and there was the ghost!

Miss Highkick-Spin screamed.
The children squealed.
Everyone hotfooted
it into the wings.

Chapter 6

Backstage, Sir Bobblysock hid up Claude's sweater. He was trembling, and desperately needed one of his long naps.

Something isn't quite right here, thought Claude, and he thought so hard that his head started to hurt.

The Viking was the next act. She had already smashed a glass and a crystal statue of a poodle when Claude saw the ghost tiptoe onto the stage behind her.

Claude looked at the ghost—from the top
of its white head to the bottom of its shoes.

That was it!
Claude wagged his
tail. None of the ghosts in his
book at home wore shoes—especially
not great big clumsy ones like that.
Ghosts *floated* daintily around, shoeless.

So if this one was wearing shoes,
it couldn't be a real ghost at all.

71

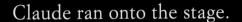

Claude ran onto the stage.

"This isn't a ghostie!" he cried.

And he grabbed the ghost's
white sheet and pulled it off.
Underneath was a naughty
man. His face was very
red and he looked
down at the floor.

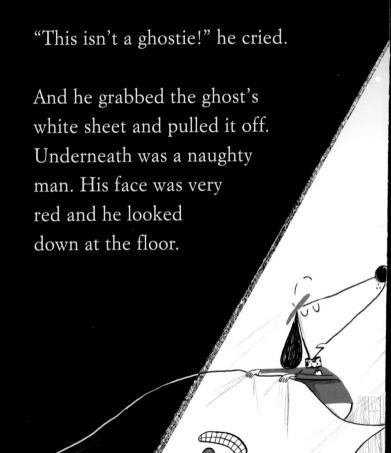

Everybody gasped
like this: *gasp!*

"What on earth are you up to?" asked Claude.

Sir Bobblysock hopped out from Claude's sweater and put his specs on so he could get a better look at the action.

"I just *love* cakes," said the naughty man, "and when I heard someone telling you that the grand prize was all the cakes you could eat, I wanted to win them. Only, I'm not very good at anything."

The audience said "Awwwww" sadly.

"So I thought if I could stop
everyone else from winning,
I could come on and do anything
and win the competition."

The audience said
"Oooooooh" crossly.

"So I went to Ida Down's Bed Emporium and bought myself this sheet and…"

Claude was just going to wag his finger at the naughty man, when—

Mr. Lovelybuns let out a yelp—
the big chandelier above his head
looked like it was about to fall!
The Viking's scream must have
set it off. If Mr. Lovelybuns didn't
move, the whole thing would
crash down on his head!

Everybody watched as the chandelier swayed. Then all of a sudden it started to fall!

Everyone panicked.
Everyone except Claude.

"Quick!" cried Claude to
the naughty man, and they
ran over to Mr. Lovelybuns.

Sir Bobblysock had a dizzy fit
and fell over with a swoon.

Claude and the naughty man stretched out the ghost's white sheet just in time and...

...caught the chandelier!

Chapter 7

B ravo!" said Mr. Lovelybuns,
clambering out of his seat.
"Claude, you saved the day. *YOU*
are the winner of the competition!"

Everybody in the theater clapped
and some even threw flowers.
Claude blushed and shyly
shook Mr. Lovelybuns's hand.
Sir Bobbysock moved to
the side on account of
his hay fever.

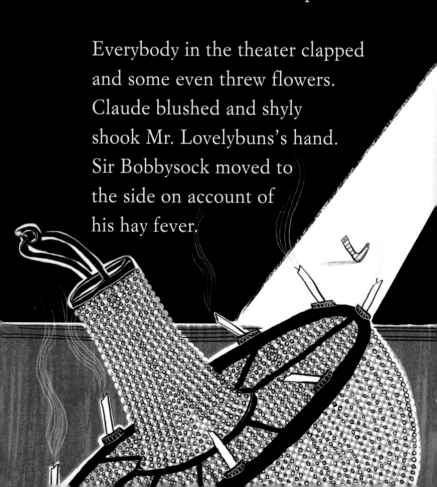

Miss Highkick-Spin fought
her way through the crowd.

"Claude," she said, with tears
in her eyes. "You are the most
wonderful dancer I've ever seen.
Won't you and Sir Bobblysock
come and travel the world with
me and dance in theaters all
over the place?"

Claude thought about
it for a moment.

Now that he'd got the hang of it,
he did rather enjoy dancing and
shaking his bottom around. But
then, he did love
living at Mr. and
Mrs. Shinyshoes's
house too.

He looked at Sir Bobblysock.
He was as white as a sheet and
looked like he had seen a hundred
ghosts. What he needed was one
of his long rests with a cup
of tea and a jelly doughnut.

Claude politely explained all of this to Miss Highkick-Spin, who understood.

Then, after saying goodbye to everyone, Claude and Sir Bobblysock made their way home, only stopping to visit Mr. Lovelybuns's Bakery.

Later that day, when Mr. and Mrs.
Shinyshoes came home from work,
they were surprised to find their
kitchen full of cakes and pastries.

"Where on earth have all these cakes come from?" said Mrs. Shinyshoes. "Do you think Claude knows anything about them?"

Mr. Shinyshoes laughed. "Don't be silly—look, he's been fast asleep all day!"

But of course Claude *did* know
where all the cakes had come from.

And we do too, don't we?

*Keep your eyes open for Claude and Sir Bobblysock.
You never know where they'll turn up next.*

CLAUDE
in the City

A visit to the city is delightful but ordinary
until Claude accidentally foils a robbery and
heals a whole waiting room full of patients!

HC: $12.95 / 978-1-56145-697-0, PB: $7.95 / 978-1-56145-843-1

CLAUDE
at the Circus

An ordinary walk in the park leads to a walk on a
tightrope when Claude accidentally joins the circus
and becomes the star of the show!

HC: $12.95 / 978-1-56145-702-1

CLAUDE
at the Beach

A seaside holiday turns out to be more than Claude
bargained for when he saves a swimmer, encounters
pirates, and discovers treasure! HC: $12.95 / 978-1-56145-703-8

CLAUDE
on the Slopes

Claude loves the Snowy Mountains—but when his
winter wonderland threatens to avalanche, he must
make a daring rescue! HC: $12.95 / 978-1-56145-805-9